Chris d'Lacey • Gus Clarke

Juggling with Jeremy

BLue Bananas

For Marshall

– Who is also quite a good weight –

Chris d'Lacey • Gus Clarke

Juggling with Jeremy

First published in Great Britain 1996 by Mammoth
an imprint of Egmont Children's Books Limited
Michelin House, 81 Fulham Rd, London SW3 6RB.
Published in hardback by Heinemann Library,
a division of Reed Educational and Professional Publishing Limited
by arrangement with Egmont Children's Books Limited.

This edition produced for The Book People Ltd
Hall Wood Avenue, Haydock, St Helens, WA11 9UL

Text copyright © Chris d'Lacey 1996
Illustrations © Gus Clarke 1996
The Author and Illustrator have asserted their moral rights.
Paperback ISBN 0 7497 2631 8
Hardback ISBN 0 434 97460 9
10 9 8
A CIP catalogue record for this title is available from the British Library.
Printed at Oriental Press Limited, Dubai.

One day Jeremy was watching T.V.

'Mu-um! I want to be a juggler!' he cried.

Mum was taking clothes
from the tumble dryer.
Some clothes were stacked on
the ironing board. She was busy.
She wasn't really listening to Jeremy.

6

Jeremy picked up three bundles of socks.

They were quite a good weight.

He started to throw the

socks into the air.

Watch this, Mum.

The socks went everywhere.

One lot dropped into the washing up –

Another lot dropped
into the dog's bowl –

Jeremy managed to catch
the other bundle.

9

Mum frowned darkly.

Jeremy blushed.

'Come on,' said Mum, 'we're going

shopping.'

But today he just wanted to juggle.

Mum bought fish and biscuits and beans.
Then she stopped by the egg counter. She
opened a box of eggs. She looked at the
eggs to check they weren't cracked.

Jeremy took three eggs. They were quite a good weight. Jeremy tossed the eggs into the air.

Oh, no. Not again!

One came down on the supermarket floor –
splat! Another came down
on the head of the supermarket
manager – double splat!

Jeremy managed to catch the other egg.

The supermarket manager was very

angry. An egg yolk was running

down his nose. It looked as if he'd got

a horrible cold.

No throwing eggs at the Manager, please!

I'm VERY angry!

Mum made Jeremy hold

onto the trolley after that.

17

On the way home, Mum stopped at

the garage to buy some petrol.

Jeremy liked the garage.

He liked to watch the petrol pumps

working. He liked to see dirty cars

going into the carwash and clean

cars coming out.

Don't make a nuisance of yourself

No chance...

But today he just wanted to juggle.

Mum went into the garage to pay for the petrol. Jeremy went with her. There was another mum there, with her little girl. The little girl was holding some cuddly toys. She had a bear, a rabbit and a chimpanzee.

Say hello to Bingo.

Jeremy frowned. He didn't think
much of cuddly toys. But he took
them anyway. He took them
outside. The toys were a good weight.
Not bad for . . .

. . . juggling.

Jeremy threw the toys into the air. The little girl laughed.

The chimp landed on the petrol station roof – *douf!*

The rabbit dropped into a passing truck – *double douf!*

Jeremy managed to catch the bear.

The little girl cried. Her mum was very angry. She didn't smile at Jeremy's mum any more. Jeremy's mum blushed. She bought the little girl a nice new rabbit from the garage display.

Little monster.

Good juggler, though!

The petrol attendant got Bingo off
the roof. Jeremy had to sit in the car
after that.

Mum was cross. 'You need a

day in the country,' she said.

'What's in the country?' Jeremy asked.

'Flowers and cows,' Mum replied.

You can't juggle flowers and cows, Mum!

I know!

Jeremy was bored. There were LOTS of flowers and cows in the country.

The farm park was brilliant.

Jeremy fed the goats and sheep from

his hands.

He watched the cows being milked.

He sat in a tractor and

steered the wheel.

But what he really

wanted to do was juggle.

Then he saw a sign that said:

Working Blacksmith

The blacksmith was putting horseshoes
on a horse. The blacksmith's name was
Tiny Tom. But he wasn't tiny.
His muscles were huge.

Tiny Tom smiled at Jeremy.

'Would you like to pass me some

horseshoes?' he said.

Jeremy picked up three horseshoes
from the pile. He held them in his
hands. They were a *very* good weight.
Just right for . . .

. . . juggling. Jeremy tossed the horseshoes in the air. One landed on the blacksmith's anvil – *crash!* Another went through the window of his workshop – *double crash!*

Jeremy managed to catch the other shoe.

Tiny Tom was very angry.

Jeremy's mum blushed. 'I'm sorry,'

she said. 'He's been doing that all day.

I wish he'd stop it.'

She told Tom about the socks and the eggs

and the toys.

'I can make him stop it,' said Tom.

Tom went across the yard.

He picked up two big sacks of

grain. He carried the grain into a

field. 'Would you like to see me juggle

these sacks?' he said.

'Yes, PLEASE!' said Jeremy.

'But you've only got two.'

'So I have,' Tom grinned. 'Now what

weighs the same as a sack of grain?'

A hundred tins of dog food?

A thousand bits of cheese?

A million mice?!

It wasn't any of these things.

It was Jeremy!

Waarrr!

Before anyone could
speak, Jeremy and
the sacks were flying
through the air.
Tiny Tom was a very
good juggler.

Va-hey!

Almost…

A sack came
down with a
thud on
the grass.

44

Jeremy sailed through the air

and landed safely

in a haystack.

Tiny Tom managed to catch the other sack.

After all that, Jeremy didn't want to juggle any more. He wanted a safer hobby. 'How about knitting?' Mum suggested. Jeremy thought that sounded boring . . .

Until he saw the balls of wool in Mum's basket!